Klassic Koalas

The Book of Valentines and Other Loves | Joanne Ehrich

KOALA JO PUBLISHING

San Mateo, California

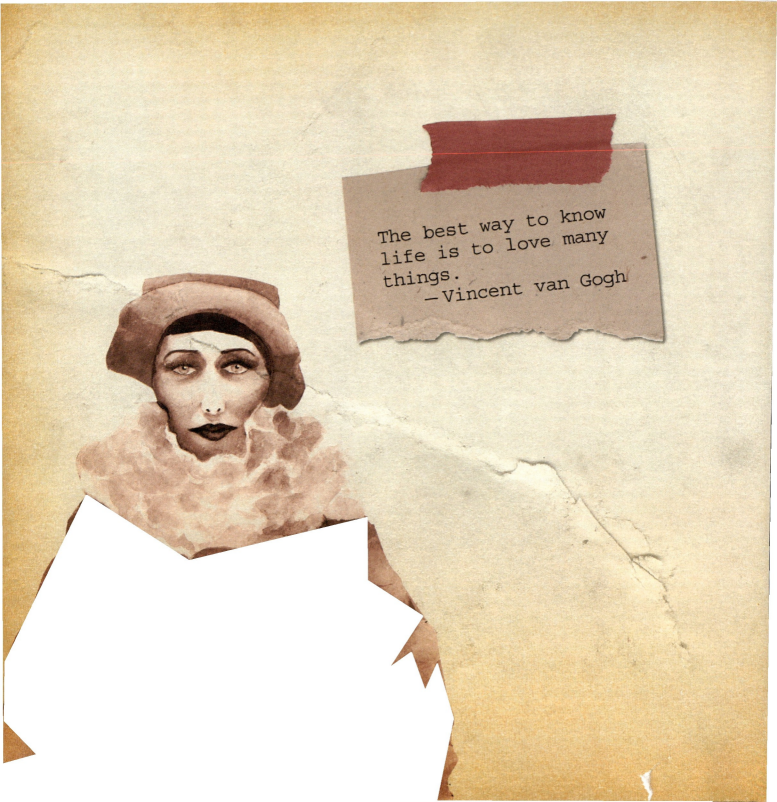

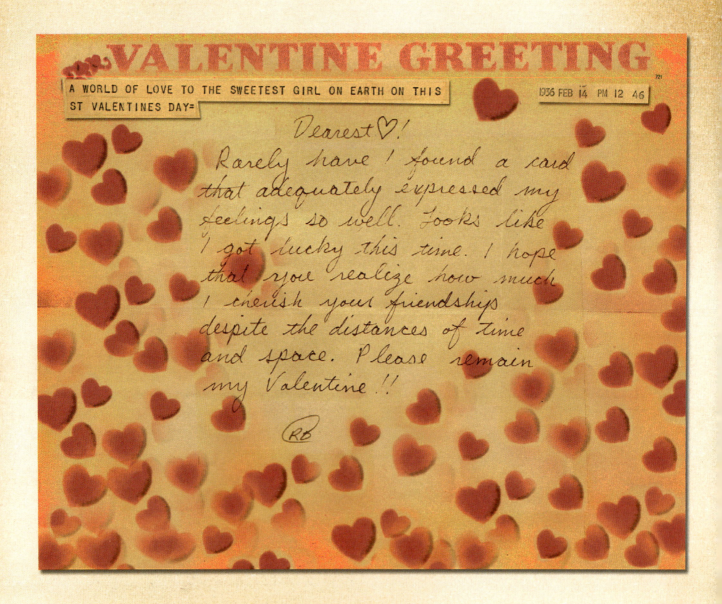

Sophie, Hermann, Eduart, Theodor

Janek

Primordial

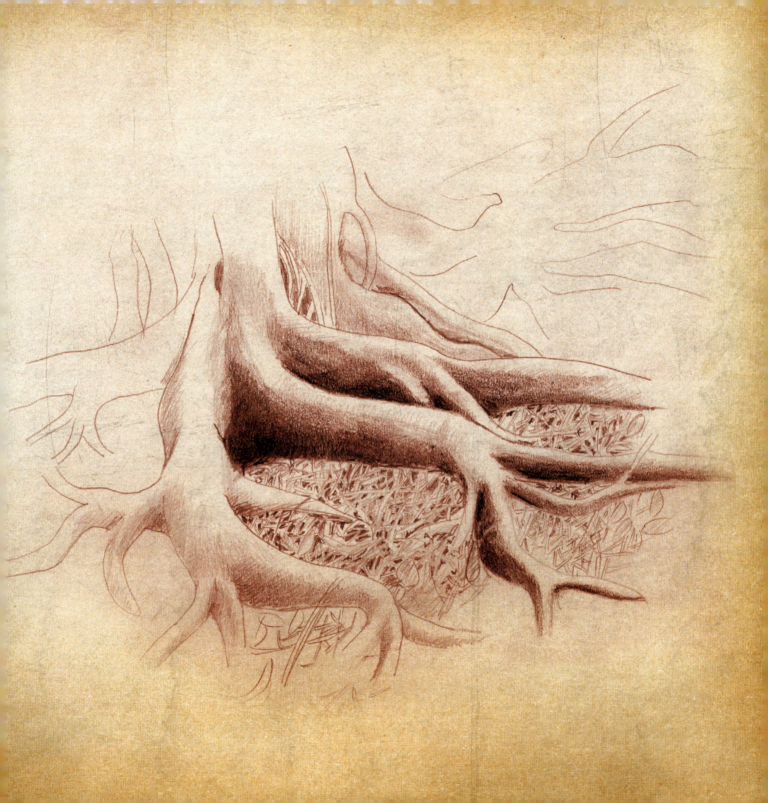

Cherished

> My beloved is only water, which is always flowing, and doesn't deceive, which is always flowing, and doesn't change, which is always flowing, and doesn't end.
> — Juan Ramon Jimenez

Creative

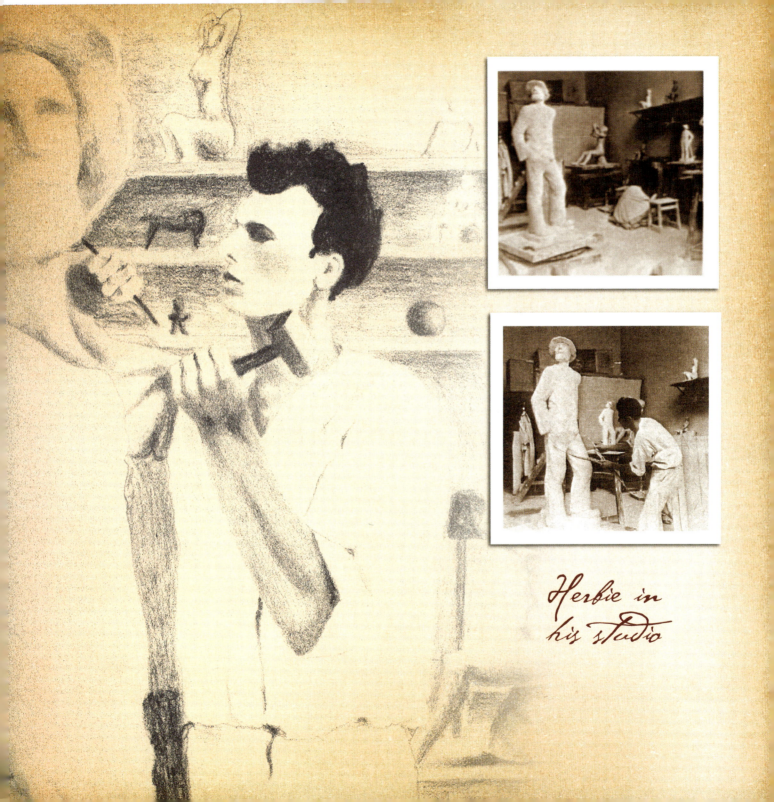

Herbie in his studio

Angelic

Together

Best Friends

Forgiving

Magic

Devoted

Dear Querida,

 I was sad to hear of your disappointments w/ the registrar's office. Can dreams be crushed so easily? I think not!! If your heart hears Europe's beckoning call, please make plans to join me for as long as you see fit.

   Love from afar,
      RB

Wide-eyed

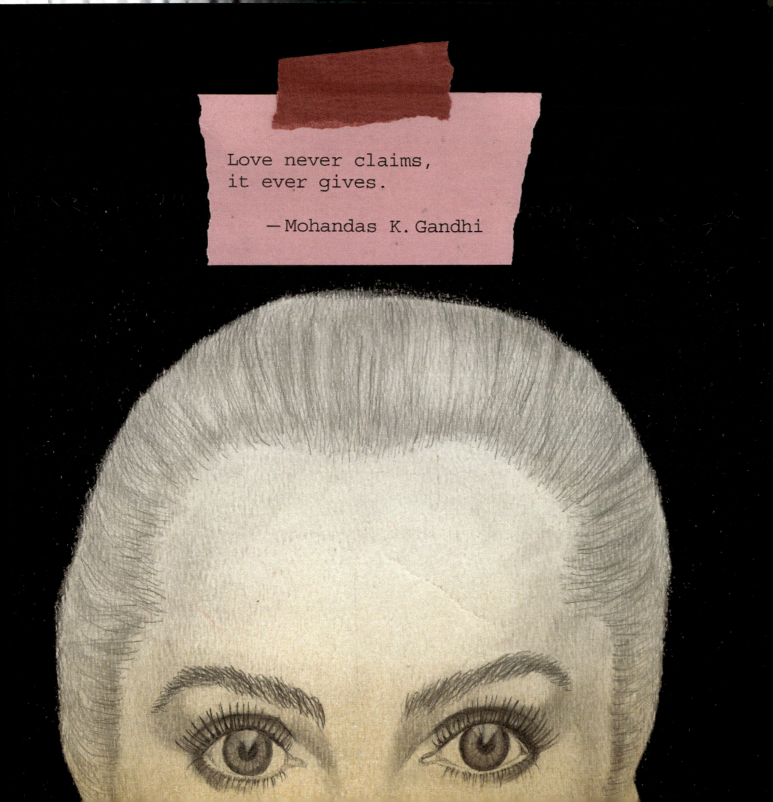

Inquisitive

Protected

From this day forward, You shall not walk alone. My heart will be your shelter, And my arms will be your home.   —Author unknown

Enchanting

Irreplaceable

Loyal

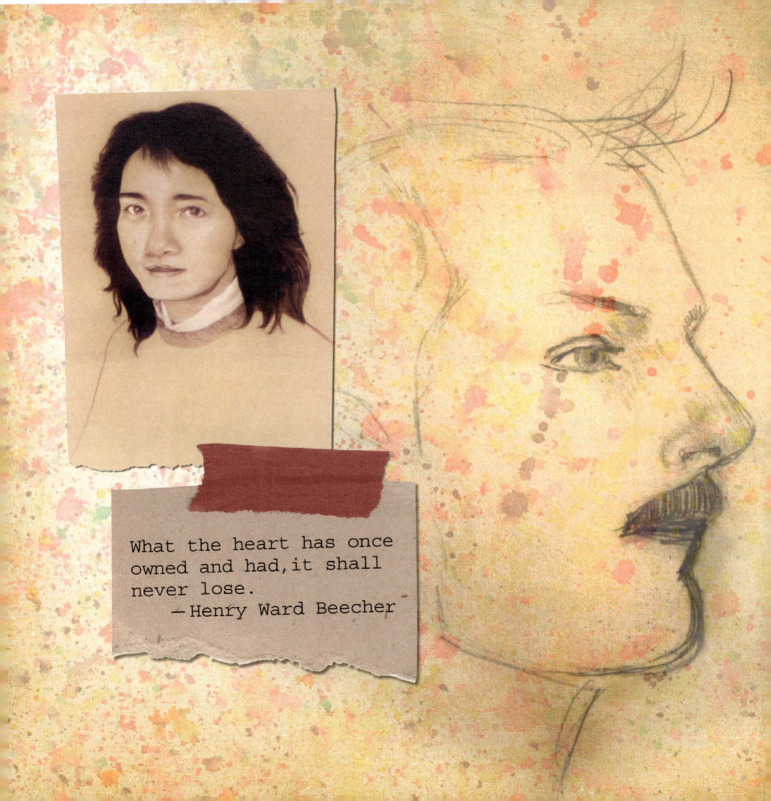

What the heart has once owned and had, it shall never lose.
— Henry Ward Beecher

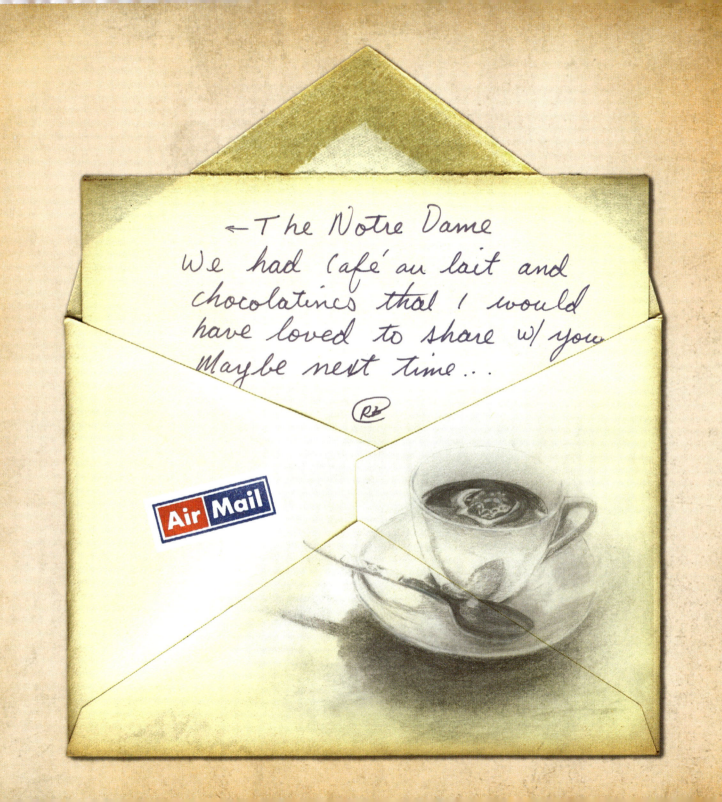

Serene

Dignified

Cara Giovanna,

    Buon Cappoanno!!! Come stai, bella? How do you like my new nick name? I think it is actually rather pretty, suits you well.

    I received your "care package" today in the mail and wanted to thank you muy pronto. I like the tie you sent, it displays your artistic respect for vivid colors. Too many of our ties are so... boring. I intend ot wear it for my next in-class presentation which will come along shortly, no doubt. I try to make my presentations rather memorable instead of those boring, comma-inducing speeches. This tie will actually look forward to them. It gives me an excellent opportunity to perfect my public speaking skills. Mustn't disappoint industry.

    I read your card carefully, several times, to get a better understanding of what you are feeling. I have always had the most peculiar feeling when I talk to you. It is as if I understand what you mean or feel without a great deal of explanation. I believe this means we are kindred spirits. This is one of those subjects that deal with emotions that are, at least for me, mightly difficult to explain. Hopefully you know what I mean.

    I believe that understanding is a prerequisite to love whether it is between a man and a woman or between fellow citizens of the world. I have been working on developing a better understanding of other people besides those I care for (such as yourself). It seems like I can get along with most everybody.

    Well, I sure hope my musings brighten up your day. At least, rest assured that you are in my thoughts.

                        With Lotsa Love and Hugs and
                          Kisses (in Abstentia),

                          Your Humble Servant and Confidant

Whimsical

Impish

Unpredictable

Magnetic

Refreshing

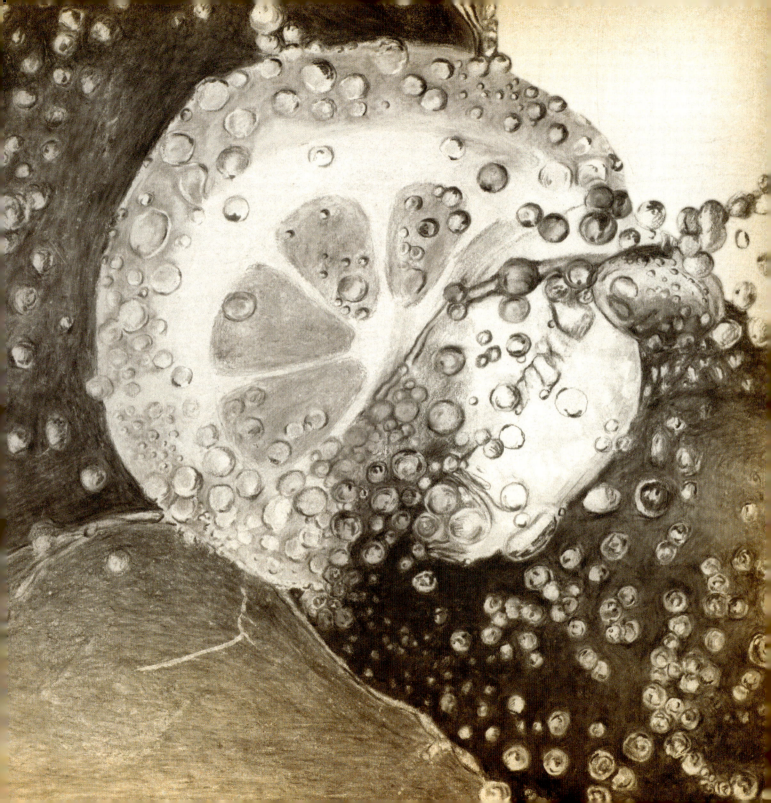

My Dearest Querida,

    I hope you don't mind me using a typewriter to ~~right~~ write as they seem so cold and unemotional but I've quite a lot to say. I hope that you received the postcard that I'd sent you from Alberta and that it wasn't too illegible.

    I'm really pleased that you returned the book and bracelet, they both mean a lot to me. That was entirely civilized of you to send them Priority Mail even though I would have been only too glad to have picked them up personally had you called me.

    I've read your letter over several times and I shall endeavour to respond to it first. It's funny but that was the only letter you've ever written me, hopefully it won't be the last.

You are the cream that will rise to the top and as soon as you realize that we will stand there together.

This world needs 110% from the likes of us if it is to survive.

    Well, having got that of my chest, I hope you will take this letter in the spirit in which it was intended. Now you must write me or I will be very cross with you!

                  With Love & Affection,

Nurturing

Everyone has a talent. What is rare is the courage to nurture it in solitude and to follow the talent to the dark places where it leads.
— Author unknown

Priceless

Curious

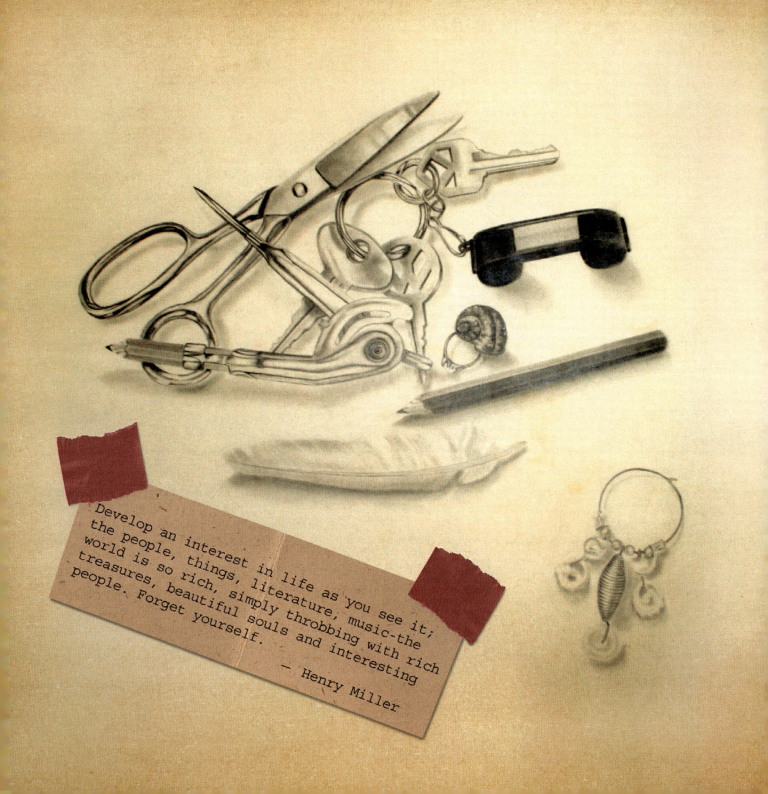

Develop an interest in life as you see it; the people, things, literature, music-the world is so rich, simply throbbing with rich treasures, beautiful souls and interesting people. Forget yourself.
— Henry Miller

Accountable

Playful

My Dearest Querida,
   Had a few weeks before school starts, so have been touring Canada. It is absolutely gorgeous here & I am quite sure you'd enjoy yourself here immensely. Have been through all the major Provincial parcs in B.C. & Alberta. Have met a lot of Brits, Germans & Canadians so am not the least bit lonely. I have seen white-tailed deer, wolves, mooses, a Raven as big as Leroy & a llama. Despite it being quite cold at night in the Rockies, I remain in high spirits. Though I miss the pleasure of your company terribly! It's just not the same w/out having someone special to share all this grandeur with. With utmost affection,
                                                                                                            R

Mesmerizing

Mysterious

Caring

Together

Eternal

The key to interpreting the pages of
Klassic Koalas: The Book of Valentines and Other Loves

The Valentines Code

A short key to interpreting the visual symbols, page by page

Van Gogh quote and Valentine letter

According to Van Gogh, the best way to know life is to love many things. Accompanied by a Valentine letter, it becomes clear that this book is not just for lovers, or koala fans.

Valentine letter and old family photo

The letter bears a date stamp from 1946, though written by modern-day RB. He knows of her fascination with all things vintage. The old photo had been added by her grandmother, Panja.

Daguerreotypes of Sophie and Janek

Panja's grandmother's images inspired Querida to draw a godly figure up in the skies. Panja's grandfather pops off the page in front of a castle drawing; here, it acts as a metaphor for her designated pantheon of ancestors.

Primordial

Blood-filled veins, accompanied by a term compatible with the universal mystery about the generations of people who preceded us and those who will follow.

Cherished

These pages feature Panja's letters, and images of sculptures Herbie made of her and others. The bright red letter seals look like cherries.

Jimenez quote and the ocean

The statue looking into the ocean survives into all eternity, like a ghostly maiden on the cliffs. Waves mimic the human heart and can make us regain our center, as true love does, when two hearts beat as one.

Creative

Here, Herbie is at work creating large sculptures inside his studio. The hand of an artist on the right mirrors the concept of creativity. Every person needs to be creative in some way.

Angelic

The young girl's copious hair envelops her face like the wings of an angel. Her innocent expression mirrors that of the angelic koala.

Together

Husband and wife are together, with each other and their friends, just like the koalas holding on to each other and the tree.

Forgiving

The seriousness of expression could be indicative of sibling rivalry, or a play on the "other woman" theme. Forgiveness heals and always benefits the forgiver as well as the forgiven.

Magic

A surreal landscape with fantastical animals encourages us to give flight to our imagination so we can create a new reality that can delight many others.

Devoted

Just as the correspondence in the envelope expresses intent to be reunited, the devoted koala opens his arm to reveal his beloved, with whom he is one.

Wide-eyed

Any relationship requires a willingness to allow oneself to be vulnerable. The lack of emotional safety, on the other hand, will disrupt the flow of energy.

Inquisitive

Find out what's beneath the surface. Looks can be deceiving – in both a negative and a positive way. Always aim at finding out who is the true individual under the clutter of pretenses.

Protected

Like a walnut shell that protects its contents, an upstanding person seeks to protect his or her beloved. Camille Claudel lived in a world in which it was difficult to find shelter.

Enchanting

Let yourself be enchanted by the true spirit and essence of another human being, in the same way that we feel an immediate attraction toward a beautiful prima ballerina.

Irreplaceable

Most people want to find that one-in-a-million person in the nameless sea of people we encounter every day, such as at a schoolyard, or on the freeway on our way to work.

Loyal

There might have been countless souls before and many after, but *the one* will always remain close to one's heart.

Notre Dame letter and Eiffel Tower

The cereal on the floor reminds us not to cry over spilled milk, even if we could have packed all our things and made our way across the Atlantic.

Serene

That girl with hair Medusa might have wanted is content to be alive in just this moment in time and no other, while absorbing the wonderful energies from all around her.

Dignified

Everyone deserves a sense of dignity, regardless of race, age, status, and species. Note the dignified expression of the stately koala, who keeps an upright pose.

Letter with Michelangelo drawing and fruit

Michelangelo's Jeremiah, the Italian fruit stand, and apples depict a zest for life and Mediterranean spirit. Behind the words is a faded rendition of Camille Claudel. Did she mirror Querida's own sadness?

Whimsical

Two fish blowing soap bubbles in a human environment in this surreal scene portray a sense of spontaneity that makes life more interesting. Whimsy can be a key to enjoying life.

Impish

Life is a dance; all the world a stage. It's good to laugh at one's own self; sometimes it's even good to "pull a leg" to lighten the mood.

Unpredictable

We all know people who have been pivotal on our path. Good friends can also be unpredictable. The toughest experiences can teach us the most valuable lessons.

Magnetic

Try to think of a universal symbol that's more magnetic than the Mona Lisa. Note the subtle spider web behind the koala. It is easy to see how one could get caught inside.

Refreshing

While biting into a lemon can make us cringe, a feeling of refreshment will follow. Do things spontaneously, without regard to what will happen next.

A letter and drawing of cognac splashing in a glass

Just as the cream will always rise to the top, a glass of cognac will always have a relaxing effect on the person who enjoys a sip.

Nurturing

An artist needs to nurture a rare talent, even if it leads into temporary darkness. There is always light at the end of a seemingly long and dark tunnel.

Priceless

Who can determine the value of a stamp that uniquely mirrors a person? Whether it be a significant other person or just a stamp, it just might be priceless.

Curious

Try to keep an open mind; the world is not just black and white, hard or soft. Consider the views of others and see what *intangible* treasures may be in store for you.

Accountable

The concentrated expression of the woman next to the open hand on the opposing page signifies both an examining mind and a sense of being accountable.

Playful

Just like the koala that may be up to some mischief, the girl and dog in this image are open to having a good time, throwing caution to the wind.

Letter and quotation about best things

An appreciation for one's surroundings and animals, despite the cold, cold weather, is evidenced on the left. This sentiment is mirrored in the quotation about the few things we need.

Mesmerizing

We might be mesmerized by the youth in this serene winter lake landscape in a way similar to how we are drawn in by this trio of special koalas.

Mysterious

Don't hunt for accolades in a desperate attempt for adoration. The mysterious will always be attractive, and inner values will pass the test of time.

Caring

There is nothing like getting together for the holidays after a long separation, and showing our appreciation for the ones we love.

United

It takes two to tango. In a similar way, we can achieve so much more with a united stand. Together, we can reach the clouds, just like the two clinging koalas.

Eternal

True love survives hurdles and may supersede the earthly plane, as symbolized by a winged nymph and a drawing with didactic Baroque elements that symbolize bodily death: a skull, a fly, dying flowers, used cigarette butts.

Other books by Koala Jo Publishing:

Klassic Koalas: Mr. Douglas' Koalas and the Stars of Qantas
Klassic Koalas: Vintage Postcards and Timeless Quotes of Wisdom
Klassic Koalas: A Coloring Book of more than 80 Koalas and Uniquely Australian Creatures
Klassic Koalas: Ancient Aboriginal Tales in New Retellings
Klassic Koalas: Vegetarian Delights Too Cute to Eat
Klassic Koalas: A Summer Party in Koalaland
Koalas: Moving Portraits of Serenity
Koalas: Zen in Fur

About the Author:

Joanne Ehrich lives in San Mateo, California, USA, where she works as a designer and illustrator. She has attended photography trade school, and holds a University degree in printmaking. She has created numerous etchings, lithographs, monotype prints, and paintings of people, animals, and landscapes. Her previous books have received rave reviews, not just for their stunning visuals and elegant layouts, but also for their loving treatment of the iconic koala.

This book is close to her heart, as it contains many references to her own personal journey. If you would like to find out more about what inspired these pages, you can download a free version of *The Valentines Code*, that includes a page-by-page key to interpreting the visual symbols and messages found throughout this book, as well as an interview with Joanne Ehrich, by flutist Viviana Guzmán. For information on how to obtain a printed hardcopy or download a free version of *The Valentines Code*, please visit www.koalajo.com/valentines.

© 2010, Koala Jo Publishing®.
Artwork © 2010, Joanne Ehrich.

Klassic Koalas™, the Koala Jo Publishing logo and name are trademarks of Koala Jo Publishing.

No part of this publication may be reproduced, stored in a retrieval system, or transmitted in any form or by any means, electronic, mechanical, photocopying, recording, or otherwise, without the prior written consent of the publisher.

Published by Koala Jo Publishing
San Mateo, Ca 94401, USA
www.koalajo.com

ISBN-10: 1441409688
ISBN-13: 9781441409683

Made in the USA
Charleston, SC
24 January 2011